Paul Jennings

*Illustrated
by Keith McEwan*

PUFFIN BOOKS

Puffin Books

Published by the Penguin Group
Penguin Books Australia Ltd,
250 Camberwell Road,
Camberwell, Victoria 3124, Australia
Penguin Books Ltd,
80 Strand, London WC2R 0RL, England
Penguin Putnam Inc.
375 Hudson Street, New York, New York 10014, USA
Penguin Books, a division of Pearson Canada
10 Alcorn Avenue, Toronto, Ontario, Canada M4V 3B2
Penguin Books (N.Z.) Ltd,
Cnr Rosedale and Airborne Roads, Albany, Auckland, New Zealand
Penguin Books (South Africa) (Pty) Ltd
24 Sturdee Avenue, Rosebank, Johannesburg 2196, South Africa
Penguin Books India (P) Ltd
11, Community Centre, Panchsheel Park, New Delhi 110 017, India

First published by Penguin Books Australia, 1994
This edition published, 2002
25 24 23 22 21 20 19
Copyright © Lockley Lodge Pty Ltd, 1994
Illustrations copyright © Keith McEwan, 1994

Designed by George Dale, Penguin Design Studio
Typeset in Palatino by Midland Typesetters, Maryborough, Victoria
Printed and bound in Australia by McPherson's Printing Group, Maryborough, Victoria

National Library of Australia
Cataloguing-in-Publication data:

Jennings, Paul, 1943–
The gizmo

ISBN 0 14 037090 0

I. McEwan, Keith II, Title.

A823.3

www.puffin.com.au
www.pauljennings.com

To Antoinette

K.M.

1

I have never stolen anything before. That's why I am not feeling so good. I think I am going to be sick all over the stall. I look at the electric gizmos all laid out for people to buy. What if I spew up just as I am taking something? What if I vomit right when I lean over the counter?

Everyone at the market will look. The police will grab me. They will tell my father. It will be in the papers. Everyone will know about the boy who was sick when he was trying to nick.

'Go on,' says Floggit. 'Don't be a wimp.' He is standing there in his stolen leather jacket. And stolen jeans. He is pointing at one of the gizmos. 'Quick, knock it off,' he says.

Why did I agree to this? Why, why, why?

'You promised,' says Floggit. He holds up the spanner that he stole from the lady on the tool stall. 'You promised to nick something if I did.'

I did promise, too. But I was just showing off. Pretending to be tough. What an idiot.

I don't want to take anything. But I promised. And Floggit will tell the kids at school that I wimped out. Broke my word. I couldn't let that happen. No way.

I swallow and try to hold down my dinner. I look at the little man who owns the stall. He is sort of strange. Like a man from another world. There is something not quite right about him. His eyes are wrong. When he blinks you can see through them as if they are windows. It seems to be raining inside his head. He looks as if he could snap his fingers and turn me into a worm. I am scared of him and I am scared of Floggit. I am too scared to steal something. And too scared not to. What will I do?

The little man bends down to tie up his shoe. It is almost as if he is daring me to take something. Behind him I see a sign that says THIEVES WILL BE PUNISHED.

'Quick,' whispers Floggit. 'This is your chance. Go, go, go.'

It is now or never. I close my eyes and grab something from the counter. I don't even know what it is. I turn and run. I scamper off like a terrified rabbit.

I hear Floggit's breath and pounding feet as he runs behind me. I run and run until my heart hurts so much that I have to stop. I collapse into a heap behind the hot-dog stall.

I wait for the screams and shouts. I wait for someone to yell, 'Stop, thief.' But no one does.

'Whoo-ee,' yells Floggit. 'You did it. You finally grew up.' He pats me on the back. 'What a hero,' he says.

Floggit grins at me. He is glad that I have done what he has done. He is glad that I am a thief like him. We both look at the gizmo which I still hold tight in my hand. It is shaped like a ball with little coloured windows in it. When I look in the windows I can see that it is raining inside. The ball is made of steel and has a button saying ON. But there is no button saying OFF. I have never seen anything that looks like this before. To be honest, it gives me the creeps.

I do not feel like a hero. I am a thief. Two minutes ago I was a normal boy. Just a kid who owned a pet mouse. And a broken bike. With the best Mum and Dad in the world. And now I am a thief. I have stolen something. And I don't even know what it is.

I feel like a worm. A worm of toothpaste that has been squeezed out of the tube and can't get back in.

'What did you get?' says Floggit. He stares at my stolen loot. 'That belongs to me,' he says. 'I get to keep it for teaching you how to flog.'

'You can have it,' I say sadly. 'I don't want it.'

'Push the ON button,' says Floggit. He does not seem quite so keen to take the gizmo now. Maybe he is scared of it.

'We don't know what it does,' I say.

'Yeah,' says Floggit. 'You'd better go back and pinch the instructions.'

A shadow falls over us. We both look up. A security guard is staring down. He wears a blue uniform. He is looking straight at us. 'Hey, you two ...' he says.

Quick as a flash, Floggit jumps up and throws the stolen spanner onto my lap. 'Here's your spanner back,' he says to me in a loud voice.

He bends down and whispers in my ear, 'Meet me at the pool.' Then he turns and runs for his life.

'Come back,' I yell. 'Don't leave me.'

Floggit looks back over his shoulder. Just for a second. 'Suffer,' is all he says. Then he vanishes around the corner.

I am left alone. With the loot. And the security guard. And a very guilty look on my face.

2

The security guard stares at Floggit as he disappears into the crowd. Then he smiles at me. 'The market is closing,' he says. 'It's time for you to go.'

'Thanks,' I mumble. I stand up and start to walk towards the gate. The gizmo and the stolen spanner seem to burn into my hands. I don't want them. I never wanted them. I feel terrible.

I do not like being a thief. I want to go back to being like before. If only I could turn the clock back. If only I could go back and unsteal the gizmo. But I can't.

Suddenly a good idea flashes into my brain. Why didn't I think of it before? I will give the gizmo and the spanner back. I will return them to the stalls and no one will know the difference. I will not be a thief any more. I am so happy that I start to smile. It is as if I have just thrown up a bad meal and feel well again.

I jog over to the tool stall. The lady is putting all of her goods into the back of a car. 'Is this yours?' I say in a trembling voice.

The lady glances at the spanner and then gives me a funny look. 'So there it is,' she says. 'I wondered where that was. I thought someone must have stolen it. Thanks.' She takes the spanner out of my hand. I go red in the face and stumble off. She thinks that I stole it. I can tell that from the tone of her voice.

Now for the gizmo. I will give it back to the man with eyes like windows. Then everything will be back to normal. I will be happy again.

I hurry over to his stall. But it is not there. The home-made cake stall is there. And the leather belt stall is there. But there is no space between them. The gizmo stall was in the middle. But now there is no middle.

'Where's the gizmo stall?' I say to the belt man.

'What gizmo stall?' he says, looking at the strange object in my hand. 'There's no gizmo stall at this market.'

He looks at me as if I am a bit crazy. And to tell the truth, I start to feel as if I am. There was a gizmo stall there but it is gone. There is not even an empty space where it was.

I turn and head out of the gate. I keep my eyes open for the little man but there is no sign of him. Not a trace.

Now what will I do? I feel sad again. Mean. I am still a thief. And I can't take the gizmo home. Dad will ask me where I got it from. I will have to make up some story. Then I will be a liar as well.

There is only one thing I can do. I can't give the gizmo back because the little man has disappeared. So I will throw it away.

I pull it out of my pocket and toss it over a fence into someone's front garden. Then I head for home.

I still feel guilty. But at least I am rid of the gizmo.

Or am I?

Something is in my pocket. Something made of steel. It is the gizmo. It is back in my pocket even though I threw it away. What is going on here? Am I going nuts? Or what?

I threw it over the fence. I know I did. And now it is back in my pocket. It won't go away. I wish I had never seen the rotten thing.

Okay. Let's see what is going on.

I put the gizmo on the footpath and watch it. Nothing happens. It just stays there. 'Goodbye,' I say. 'Goodbye for good.' I start to back away along the footpath. I don't take my eyes off the gizmo. And it doesn't move.

Finally I reach a corner. I turn round and run like crazy. I go like the wind. I am the fastest runner in the whole school and if anyone can get away from the gizmo it is me. I pelt up the road and along to the railway bridge. When I reach the bridge I stop and pat my pocket.

The gizmo is back inside.

3

The gizmo is like a guilty conscience. You can't get rid of it. Just when you think everything is all right – there it is again making you feel bad.

I stand on the bridge and look down onto the tracks. A train is coming. A goods train pulling carriages filled with coal.

I take out the gizmo and hold it out over the tracks. The train roars by way below. 'Goodbye,' I say. I let the gizmo drop. It spins down and down and falls into an open coal carriage.

Straight away I start to feel better. Now I can go home and forget about one of the worst days of my life. Tomorrow is a school day. Floggit will want his spanner back. Too bad. He ran off and left me to face the security guard. If he calls me a wimp I will have a few things to say to him.

I start to make a speech in my mind. 'Floggit,' I say to myself. 'You are a coward. You ran away and left me to get caught.' I know really

that I will never say this to Floggit because he is big and tough and will flatten me if I even blink an eyelid at him. Still, it doesn't hurt to dream.

My daydream is suddenly interrupted. I feel something in my pocket. Oh no. The gizmo. It is covered in coal dust. It is back. And it is mine for ever. There is just no getting rid of it.

Maybe if I press the ON button again it will go away. Carefully I put my thumb on the button and press it. The gizmo starts to hum very softly but nothing else happens. It is very disappointing. Then, after about twenty seconds it gives a loud 'beep' and falls quiet.

A tall man who is jogging along in a tracksuit gives me a stare as he goes by. He looks a bit funny in his outfit. Red and yellow socks don't really go with purple pants. He looks about as silly as I feel.

What am I going to do with the gizmo? It can't stay in my pocket for the rest of my life. And what about when I have a shower? What will happen to it then? Will it stay stuck to me or will it stay in the pocket of my jeans?

I decide to find out. I reach home and sneak in the back door and up to my bedroom. I pull off my jeans and throw them, with the gizmo, into the corner. Now we will see whether or not it stays in the pocket.

It does. Nothing happens. But something is wrong. Something is not quite right. I am wearing a pair of red socks with a yellow band. But mine don't have a yellow band.

The hair starts to stand up on the back of my head. Where did these socks come from? I am sure that I was wearing plain ones this morning.

This is nutty. Really weird. What is going on here?

I have to get away from this gizmo. It is driving me crazy.

I pull on my jeans and go out into the back yard. I get a spade and start to dig. The ground is hard. After an hour of digging I have only made a shallow hole. I keep going. The sweat pours down my face. My fingers are blistered. I have never worked this hard before in my life. Finally the hole is as deep as the handle of the shovel.

I drop the gizmo into the bottom of the hole and shovel in dirt like mad. Just to be on the safe side I toss in a couple of rocks. Then I stand back and look. The gizmo is gone. Dead and buried.

I decide to say a few words over the burial plot. I mean it is a sort of funeral. It is only right and proper to say something. I bow my head. 'Gizmo,' I say. 'Rest in peace. And let me live in peace. I know I should not have stolen you. But I have learnt my lesson. You stay down there and I will stay up here. Amen.'

I walk out of the gate and down to the shops. I feel a lot better. Until I hear a soft buzzing noise. I pat my pocket and feel the gizmo inside. It is all covered in dirt and humming softly.

4

'Shoot,' I say with a groan. 'The gizmo is back.'
I feel like I am having a terrible nightmare.

There is a big man standing nearby. He is
huge. And tough looking. He stares at me as if
I am a bit mad. Talking to myself like that.
Suddenly two things happen. The gizmo beeps.
And the tough guy falls to the ground and
starts screaming. He is yelling and howling in
agony.

He is pulling at his feet. Trying to get his shoes off. 'Ouch, ow, aagh.' He pulls off one shoe and then starts on the next. But it won't budge.

What has happened to the poor guy? I have had a stone or two in my own shoes but I have never carried on like this. His face is screwed up in agony. Tears are squeezing out of his eyes. 'Get it off, get it off,' he yells. He is waving his shoe at me as if it is filled with hot lead.

I rush over and grab his shoe. It is on tight. Terribly, horribly tight. The laces are undone but the shoe won't budge. I pull and strain and struggle. Suddenly it comes off with a pop and I fall over backwards.

I look at the shoe. Then I drop it in fright. A cold feeling comes all over me. The shoe is about ten times too small for his huge foot. I have seen a shoe like this before. It is like my own.

It is my own.

I stare down at my feet. I am wearing a pair of boots that are about ten sizes too big for me. And I am not the only one staring at them. The big guy grabs me and lifts me up by the ankles. I am hanging there like a dead chook. He shakes me up and down, pulls off the boots and drops me onto my head. It hurts like crazy.

The big guy stomps off down the road. 'I don't know how you did that,' he says. 'But it wasn't funny. Not funny at all.'

I pick up my own shoes and put them back on. He was right. This is not a funny situation. I am in big trouble. I just don't know what to do.

I sit down and think. When the gizmo starts to hum it means trouble. It hums for about twenty seconds. Then it beeps. Then I get a bit of the nearest person's clothes. And they get a bit of mine. The striped socks must have come from the jogger. I went home with his and he ran off with mine. I give the ON button another press. It makes a squealing noise. I hope I have not made things worse. But I think I have.

I must get rid of the gizmo. It just keeps returning to its owner. No it doesn't. I am not its owner. I am its stealer. And I am in big trouble. Finally I get it. Finally I realise what is going on. The gizmo will always return to the person who stole it.

I will have to go back and tell Dad. He will know what to do. But he will give me a big lecture. He will go on and on about stealing. I will never hear the end of it. I look around for someone to help. Give me a bit of advice.

Down the street I can see a cloud of flies. Under the flies is a tramp. He wears a battered old hat that looks like a half-opened can of beans. He has whiskers. And an old coat with holes in it. And trousers with the knees showing through. He is whistling and walking along with his dog.

The tramp has a kind face. He looks like he has been around. Seen a few things. Maybe he can help. Maybe he has come across a gizmo before. I head off in his direction.

'Hey,' I say. 'Have you ever heard of a gizmo?' I hold it up for him to see.

The tramp gives a grin and shows his yellow teeth. He looks at the gizmo which begins to hum even louder than before.

'Oh no,' I yell. 'No, no, no.' I turn and start to run down the street. I throw the gizmo into the air. I hear it beep. Suddenly I fall. I trip over my long trousers. The ones with the hole in the knee.

5

I tumble along the road and stop in the gutter. I have grazed my knee and it stings terribly. I sit up and see the tramp heading off in the other direction. 'Thanks,' he yells. 'Thanks a lot. They're a bit tight, but they'll do.'

He is wearing my new jeans. And my best windcheater. And my shoes.

I have a hat on that looks like a half-opened can of baked beans. And I am dressed in a smelly old suit. I look inside. I even have his underpants on. They are all stained and horrible. The sort that your grandfather wears, all floppy and loose.

'Come back,' I scream. 'Come back, thief.'

The tramp is moving off as fast as he can go. 'Thanks,' he says again. 'Thanks a lot.' He is chuckling to himself. He thinks it is Christmas. His lucky day.

And my unlucky one.

I hitch up my old trousers and hobble after him. 'You wait,' I yell. 'You just wait.' It is tough talk but to be honest I don't know what I am going to do when I catch him. He looks like he has seen a lot of life. He could flatten me for sure. Still and all, I have to try and get my clothes back. Dad gets really mad if I even tear my shirt. You wouldn't know what he would do if I lost everything. This is really bad.

The tramp disappears around a corner. By the time I turn it he is nowhere to be seen. The street is full of people who are coming out of a church. It is a wedding and all the people are dressed in their best clothes and throwing confetti.

'He is hiding,' I say to myself. 'The tramp is hiding in the crowd.' I start to push through the people trying to find the tramp.

'Go away,' sniffs a lady as I push past her legs. 'Dreadful boy. Smelly. Awful. How dare you dress like that at a wedding. Go away.'

I pretend not to hear. I have to get my clothes back or Dad will kill me. Suddenly I find myself staring at the bride. She is beautiful. Lovely. Nearly as good as my girlfriend Kate. She wears a veil in her hair. And flowers. And a long white dress.

Two little kids in purple are holding a long train out at the back. Her new husband is standing next to her, all dressed up to kill. I recognise him. He is the coach of our local football team. At the back is the preacher. His head nearly falls off when he sees me and my outfit.

The bride looks at me. And I look at her. She is shocked to see a boy dressed like a tramp.

Suddenly there is a hum. It is coming from my pocket. 'No, no, please no,' I scream. The crowd are all looking at me. Everyone falls silent. The gizmo beeps.

And the bride is dressed like a tramp.

And I am dressed like a bride.

She opens her mouth and screams in horror. I open my mouth and scream in horror. We both scream and scream and scream at each other. There is a flash of light. A photographer is taking photos of me. I can't have this. It will be in the paper. Me, Stephen Wilkins, dressed like a bride.

I turn and push my way through the crowd. The open road is in front of me. 'Get him,' yells someone. 'Get the little beggar.'

They are after me. The preacher, the two little pageboys in purple. The bride and groom. The whole crowd.

I hobble along as fast as I can. This is no good at all. I can't run fast. They are catching up to me. I bend down and take off my high-heel shoes. Much better. I bolt along the road with no shoes. But the stones are hurting me. My feet start to bleed. The angry mob is catching up.

6

They will tear me to pieces if they get me. 'Oh help, help. Someone please help.' The bride is foaming at the mouth. She doesn't want a photo album filled with pictures of a lady tramp marrying a football coach.

'Help,' I say to myself. 'Someone help.'

But there is no one. Only a horse tied to a rail. It is Kate's horse. She is always on at me to have a ride on her horse Tiffany. She won't mind if I borrow her horse.

I have never ridden a horse before but it can't be that hard. Can it?

I try to jump up onto the saddle. The bride's outfit is too baggy. It gets in the way. I can't get up. My bra is twisted. My pantyhose are coming off and my knickers are slipping.

Oh, the shame of it. A boy in a bride's outfit.

But there is no time to be embarrassed. The bridal party is coming. And they are not throwing confetti. They are hurling insults. 'Grab him. Quick,' yells the football coach.

Just as they are about to grab me I manage to scramble up onto the horse. 'Go,' I say, 'Go, go, go.'

The horse just stands there. How do you get horses to go? I don't know. The groom lunges for me. He trips and falls. The horse rears up. Then it bolts.

'Stop,' I yell. 'Stop.' The horse is galloping flat out. How do you get horses to stop? I don't know. It charges along the main street. Its hooves pound the road like a million mallets. Everyone stops to look. People jump out of the way. Cars screech to a halt. My bridal train is streaming out behind me. My veil swirls over my head.

Like a mad ghost at midnight I gallop down the street. Out of the town. Down the highway. Up and down. Jogging around. I am dead. I know I am dead. The ground is wheeling by. Trees speed past me. The horse charges at some trees. Through branches that whip and scratch my face. Blood is trickling onto my long white dress. My veil is torn to shreds. I have confetti up my nose. 'Save me. Someone please save me,' I snort.

We are galloping up a steep, grassy bank. Just below is the local swimming pool. Kids are jumping off the diving board. Others are sunbaking. But to me they are all a blur.

Suddenly the horse puts on the brakes. It just stops and I go flying over its head. Up I go. Up and over.

Everything turns black.

7

I am dead.

No, I'm not. There is grass in my mouth. And in my eyes. I am stiff and sore but I am not dead.

I am upside down on the grass. Inside the pool fence.

Nearby is a girl. She is staring at me with wide open eyes.

I blink and rub the dirt out of my eyes. The girl looks as if she has never seen a boy before. I guess she hasn't. Not one dressed in a bridal dress who has just flown over the fence.

She is wearing a baby-pink bikini.

My head is spinning so much that I can hardly see her. I am confused. I can't think straight. There is a buzzing sound in my ears.

Then a beep.

'No, no, no. Not a bikini. Agh ... '

The girl is screaming. I am screaming. The bikini does not suit me. Not at all. The girl looks down at her wedding gown. She hasn't a clue where it came from. She races into the changing rooms as quick as she can go. I look around for the boys' showers. Where are they? Where, oh where? People are staring at me. A boy in a bikini. Shame.

I pull off the top part of the bikini and toss it away. At least I am rid of the bra bit. But I still look ridiculous. The bottom part of the bikini keeps slipping. The gizmo is pulling it down. This is a nightmare.

I can hear laughing. Girls laughing. About thirty of them. They are all dressed in the uniform of the Loreto Convent. They are filing through the turnstiles. They are going past the door to the boys' showers. I am trapped. Where can I go? I can't let the Loreto Girls see me like this. There is nowhere to go. Except up.

The diving board. It is the only way. If I climb up there maybe I can lie down and no one will see me. I start to climb as fast as I can go. I hope like crazy that my bikini bottom holds. If it slips I am done for.

'Hey,' says a loud voice.

Oh no, now I am in for it.

'Sh,' I say. 'Please be quiet.'

Then I see who it is. Someone dressed in jeans and a leather jacket. Someone who has a part-time job at the pool. He is not going to be quiet. No way. Never. He is going to talk in a loud voice. He is going to show off in front of the girls. It is Floggit. He is going to make sure that everyone in the world sees me up there in my bikini.

8

'Where have you been, little wimp?' says Floggit. 'I have been waiting for you. Where is my spanner? And my gizmo.'

His eyes grow wide when he sees the tiny pink bikini. 'What are you wearing that for?' he says. 'Are you nuts or something?'

He looks at the gizmo that is bulging out of my bikini bottom.

'Where's the spanner?' he growls.

'I gave it back to the lady,' I whisper.

All my strength is gone. I just can't take any more. I can't stand up to him. I panic and keep climbing.

Floggit decides to make sure that the whole world sees me. 'Look at this,' he yells.

My heart misses a beat. The girls have seen me in my bikini. They all gather around. Looking up and laughing at the sight. How embarrassing.

It is a long way down. But I can't stay up there with everyone watching.

DIVING
BOARD

How can I escape? There is nowhere to go but down. It is a long way. I close my eyes and jump.

Kersplash. The water gurgles around me. And above me. I hold my breath and slowly start to float up. Now what will I do? I am in the pool where no one can see my bikini. But I will have to get out some time.

As I float up I get an idea. A very good idea. It is a risk. The biggest risk of all time. But I will do it.

I burst up into the sunlight and gulp in air. Then I slowly swim to the edge of the pool.

Floggit is there waiting for me.

I grab the side of the pool, the gizmo in one hand.

'I'll take this, wimp,' says Floggit. He snatches the gizmo from me.

My heart feels light. It worked. He has stolen the gizmo. It is his now. And he can keep it.

I climb out of the pool. The girls stand there looking at me and my pink bikini. They giggle at me but I don't care any more. Something good is going to happen. If my plan works.

Right on cue the gizmo starts to hum. At any moment it will beep. I will get Floggit's outfit and he will get mine.

9

Before Floggit can say a word there is a beep. I have to time this just right. I turn my back on the crowd. I take off my bikini and throw it over the fence. I am naked. But only for a flash.

The gizmo beeps.

I get Floggit's outfit and he gets mine.

I am fully dressed in a leather jacket and jeans. I have Floggit's gear. And he has what I was wearing. Nothing. He is starkers. Not a stitch on. He tries to cover himself up with his hands. He is babbling and squealing in fright.

He doesn't know what is going on. He tries to hide. But there is nowhere to hide.

Floggit screams and screams. The girls start to laugh when they see him. They think it is an enormous joke. Floggit stares at the gizmo in his hand. He shrieks and throws it away as if it is red hot. But it just comes back to him. He turns and runs. He goes for his life and the gizmo follows. Like a guilty conscience.

Floggit is scared of the gizmo. Terrified.

He heads for the diving board. Up he goes. And after him goes the gizmo, bouncing from step to step. Floggit stands on the top of the board shivering and trying to hide his naked body from the girls. He blubbers and bawls but there is nowhere to hide. The whole world can hear him. In the end he jumps.

The gizmo follows. It does a perfect dive.

The girls all stand on the edge. They think it's a great joke. Floggit treads water out in the middle. He will have to come out sooner or later. He can't stay there all day.

And neither can I. It is time for me to go.

'Come back,' Floggit yells. He does not sound tough at all. Just the opposite in fact. I don't think he will ever bother me again. 'Don't leave me,' he calls.

I look back over my shoulder. Just for a second. 'Suffer,' I say. Then I run off as quickly as I can. As I go I think I see a little man with eyes like windows. He is looking at Floggit and chuckling.

When I reach home I think about what I will do with Floggit's leather coat and jeans.

I decide that I will give them back to him in the morning. Might as well. After all, I don't want people saying I'm a thief.

Do I?